W9-DIB-418

SKY FULL OF BABIES

Story
by Richard
Thompson

Art
by Eugenie
Fernandes

Annick Press Ltd.   Toronto, Ontario

Annick Press
All rights reserved

Third Printing, February, 1988

Graphic realization and
design by Eugenie Fernandes

Annick Press gratefully acknowledges
the support of The Canada Council
and The Ontario Arts Council

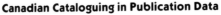

Canadian Cataloguing in Publication Data
Thompson, Richard 1951–
  Sky full of babies

(The Jesse adventures)
ISBN 0-920303-93-5 (bound) ISBN 0-920303-92-7 (pbk.)

I. Fernandes, Eugenie, 1943–   . II. Title.
III. Series: Thompson, Richard, 1951–   . The
Jesse adventures.

PS8589.H65S57 1987   jC813'.54   C87-094085-6
PZ7.T46Sk 1987

Distributed in Canada and the USA by:
Firefly Books Ltd.
3520 Pharmacy Ave. Unit 1c
Scarborough, Ontario
M1W 2T8

Printed and bound in Canada
by D.W. Friesen & Sons Ltd.

To Jesse

Jesse built a spaceship right in the middle of her room.

"Come in my spaceship, dad," she said.

"Okay," said her dad. He had to share a seat with Jesse's baby, but that was alright.

"Where are we going?" he asked.

"Space," replied Jesse.

"Of course…," said her dad.

"Do up your seat belt," said Jesse.

He did.

"I have some cocoa, and I have some milk," said Jesse. "Do you want some?"

"Sure," said her dad.

"I don't like cocoa," said Jesse.

"I'll have the cocoa," said her dad.

Jesse handed her dad a steaming cup of hot cocoa. He sipped it carefully.

"Captain Jesse," he said, "what will we see in Space?"

Jesse finished her milk and licked off the mustache.

"A lady with flowers in her hair," she said.

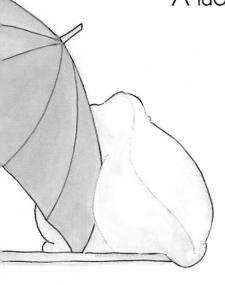

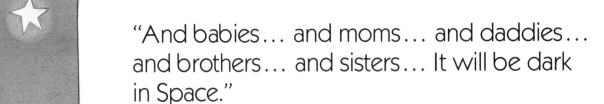

"And babies... and moms... and daddies... and brothers... and sisters... It will be dark in Space."

"What are all those people doing in Space?" asked her dad in surprise.

"They are giving the babies lots of hugs," said Jesse. "Then they are putting them to bed."

"Then what?" asked her dad.

"Then it gets to be morning. When it is morning it is time to blast off to home."

Jesse grasped the steering wheel.

"Hold onto the baby!" she called. "BLAST OFF!"

The engines roared! Smoke and steam bellowed around them! The cup trembled in its saucer! The window shook! The pictures on the wall rattled!

They were off!

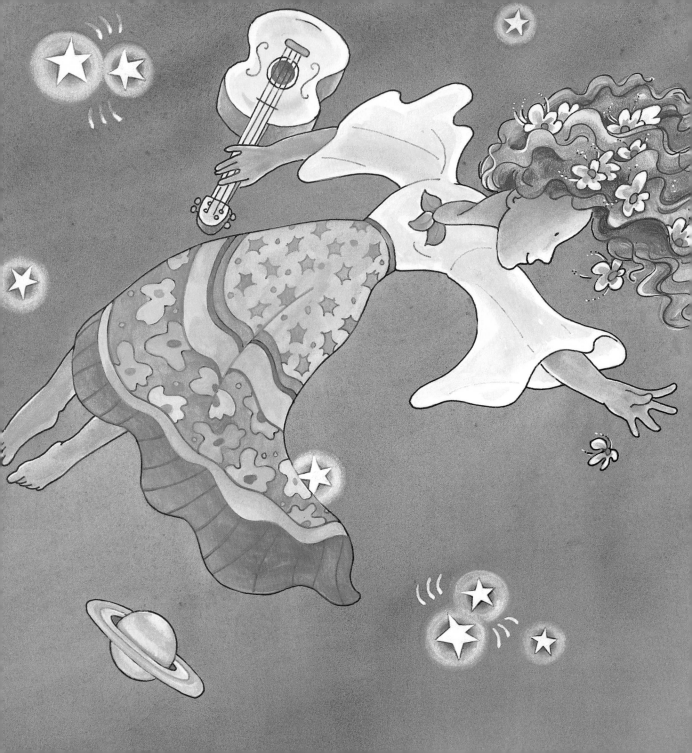

When they got to Space, it was dark—just as Jesse said it would be. Not completely dark, of course. Stars and planets winked and shone. The stars bumped together gently, with a soft tinkling that sounded almost—almost—like "Twinkle Twinkle Little Star."

"There she is!" said Jesse.

And there she was—the lady with flowers in her hair—just like Jesse said she would be. She waved to them as they passed.

Suddenly, a baby floated by the spaceship—then another, and another. The sky was full of babies. They laughed and cooed. They wiggled their fingers and kicked their feet. They sucked on their fists and made little spit bubbles.

A dad and a mom drifted by.
A brother and a sister tumbled past.
It was just like Jesse said it would be!

Whenever a mom got close
to a baby, she would reach out
and take the baby in her arms
and give that baby a big hug.
Dads and brothers and sisters
were all busy, too— hugging babies.

Jesse's dad heard a gentle singing sound around them. At first he thought it was just the tinkling of the stars, but it got louder.

"The lady with the flowers in her hair is singing a lullaby," said Jesse. "It is sleeping time."

And sure enough, every mom or dad was holding a baby and rocking it gently, or patting its back, or rubbing its tummy—whatever made the baby happy. The singing filled the space all around. The babies all closed their eyes.

Jesse's dad got sleepier and sleepier. His head began to nod. His eyes closed. He slept peacefully—like a baby in space. Jesse steered the ship on and on and on.

When her dad finally woke up, they were close to the sun.

"It is almost morning, dad," said Jesse. "Time to blast off to home."

The engines roared softly, and the spaceship leapt ahead ...

They got home just as Jesse's mom was coming into the room.

"We just got back from Space," Jesse's dad told her as he unbuckled his seat belt and stepped out of the ship.

"That sounds exciting!" said her mom. "Can I come with you next time, Jesse?"

"Sure," said Jesse, "Want to go now?"

"Well, let's see…"

"Ah, go ahead," said Jesse's dad.

Jesse's mom got into the ship.
"I have some cocoa, and I have some milk,"
said Jesse. "Want some?"